Malabar Mind

Praise for Malabar Mind

'From marmalade mornings, sun dried memories, cow-like grey clouds to the shy raindrop — her new medium of thought takes you to another plane, where words paint pictures and fantasy takes wing. The mundane business of living takes on a fresh perspective in her hands, stringing lust, hope, anguish, joys in its wake'

— *The Times of India*

'Words have befriended Anita Nair, giving wing to an imagination which helps express the idiosyncrasies of everyday life'

— *The Asian Age*

'...poetry that grapples, twists and turns with contemporary existence. *Malabar Mind* is an interesting collection, to be read with pleasure and occasionally delight'

— *The Sunday Express*

'Anita has a remarkable body language of variegated repetitions which comes through well as a narrative even in very short poems giving a local habitation and a name to passing thoughts'

— *The Sunday Herald*

'Anita Nair's first book of poems *Malabar Mind* is impossible to get away from'

— *The Hindu Literary Supplement*

'...wide-ranging and acutely observed'

— *Outlook Magazine*

'Her poems are deeply rooted in the South Indian landscape — full of gods, myths, colour, heat, and the tropical profusion of the terrain'

— *Poetrymagazines.org.uk*

Malabar Mind

Anita Nair

HarperCollins *Publishers* India

First published in India by
HarperCollins *Publishers* in 2011
Building 10, Tower A, 4th Floor, DLF Cyber City, Phase II,
Gurugram Haryana – 122002, India
www.harpercollins.co.in
This edition published in India in 2020 by HarperCollins *Publishers*

2 4 6 8 10 9 7 5 3 1

P-ISBN: 978-93-5357-618-9
E-ISBN: 978-93-5357-619-6

Typeset in 11.5/14 Adobe Thai
Jojy Philip New Delhi 110015

Printed and bound at
MicroPrints India, New Delhi

For B

*For years of love, laughter, claws, fangs,
breath, memories, blood, tears, stars, buds, hurt,
hope, dreams, life.*

Contents

Mostly a Man. Sometimes a God

Know this, woman
Clasped around my forearm are a thousand suns.
The mark of who I am
Mostly a man, sometimes a God.
Crawling, marauding
I feel your eyes
Trace vermilion, turmeric and rice paint paths
Slashing the brown silk of my skin.
Woman, I feel your touch.

The debris of light;
The density of a starless night.
My forefinger my brush,
Glistening lamp black my paint.
When your eyes meet mine
In the mating pool of the mirror,
My hand falters,
The line smudges.
Woman, you do not know what you do to me.

Woman, I have shed my skin.
I have sipped at timelessness.
Now I shall cease to be.
But before you diminish
Into nothingness,
I savor the life juice of the coconut palm.
Cup the baked earthen pot as if it were your chin.

I wet my lips at your mouth.
I drink deep of this forbidden mortal desire.

My crown is wrought of grass and divinity.
Fat lips, white lips, wool fuzz hide my adulterous mouth.
I sling the bamboo bow.
And raise the gleaming blade.
Drums throb to awaken the slumbering god.
Anklets shiver as the man in me retreats.
I am no longer who you desired.
I am your protector.
The fierce god Muthappan.

Muthappan *speaks*:
I'm lord of the jungle, son of the tortured vines
Fleet of foot, loyal to the last.
The dog is my comrade,
The blind Thiruvappan my companion.
Through the dark times of this age
I shall be with you.
To help and console.
To provide and protect.

Look, with this arrow
That pierces the eye of the coconut
I destroy all evil
That swirls around you.
I pluck from the crown of hope.
Fragments for you to build
Your dreams upon.
I press my palm on your head;
Let your nerve ends carry this message
That I shall never forsake you.

All this and more
I shall do for you.
But first there is a thirst in me
That I shall quench with milk still warm.
With toddy that bubbles
Unable to still time.
I suck on the long bronze spout
I crunch a piece of dried fish
Muthappan is satisfied;
Muthappan is happy.

Muthappan has spoken.
He no longer needs me.
My crown of power is of wilted grass.
The salt of sweat runs down my brow.
With fingers that had once sought perfection,
I wipe away the guise of divinity.
Woman, I am once again who I was,
A man with skin and eyes
That seek yours.

Woman, let me match my longing with yours.
Let me sear your lips with mine.
Let me burn your flesh with my hunger.
Why then do you evade me now?
Is it that you smell the savage?
Is it that you fear who I was?
Woman listen,

I am a man;
Only sometimes a god.

May You Sleep a Million Years, Shiva

I

Lord of the universe
Master of destruction,
I stand before you
Unwilling to be cowered.

Have you ever felt
The bones of your child prod your palm?
Have you ever heard
The piercing wail of hunger?

II

I have appeased
The demands of my calling.
I have chanted your name
A million times and more.

And yet, my ancestors will return
Ghouls hungry for the crumbs of my guilt.
For they know when I forsake you
I forsake them.

III

I shall no longer gather shoe flowers,
Hide the blackness of your tumescence

With the red petals of hope
That bud, blossom and die in these courtyards.

No lamp will burn as your all seeing eye.
No camphor breath of yours will singe these walls.
Never again will I pretend that you exist.
Your blessings are ashes that stick in my throat.

IV

One last time
I plunged into the green pond.
Slime infested tears of men chosen as I was.
One last time I held the thread that bound you to me.

Let this then be my parting curse:
May you live trapped in your slumber.
And when I am gone, none shall awaken you
No bells shall ever ring for you.

Vulcan in Brindavan

Paul the Czech never came.
He arrived
Armed for the tropics in his solar topi
Mosquito nets, insect repellents
A pocket book and blue searching eyes.

Communism is a myth.
You live in fear of the secret police, the army.
Equality is a tall tale.
In India, you don't know what fear is
What it is to be thwarted at every step
Until you learn to swill frustration in vodka
The patriot's drink.
True, true, we exclaimed in horror.

Paul the madman
Throwing buckets of water
On the brown hard earth
Coaxing grass to grow,
Green, moist and rampant.

Vedas are crap.
Did you know Vatsyayana was a celibate?
Isn't Krishna's colour blue?
Blue, the colour of infinity, eternity.
We discovered Kathakali
Seated cross-legged at Paul's side

Paul wrapped our heritage with foreign awe
And gifted it back to us.

Paul knew Martina
When she swung tennis balls
Across nets with the famous back-hand.
In that world Paul discovered atoms,
Their follies and foibles.

Why do you deify everyone?
From your town clerk to the lord mayor.
Why do you offer bribes?
Vehemence, more of it at such passiveness.
Your national animal ought to be the cow,
We shake our heads, we don't know,
Our excuse: maybe it is because the British
Ruled us for three hundred years.

Paul called our Priyadarshini a queen
a megalomaniac tottering at her end.
We nearly slit his throat.
So what if he knew much more than us?
We don't accept that kind of talk from a foreigner.

Vulcan in Love

Remember Paul,
Vulcan whose tongs threw sparks in Brindavan.
Paul flew from the Peninsula
Across the equator,
On the trail of Magellan
Stars on this side of Capricorn shine brighter,
He said.
Paul discovered another paradise,
The old one had turned stale.
Women who fed him rice cakes and stew,
Craved for non-stick frying pans
French perfume
And pleaded,
No space for you. Sorry.

Unni, the bearded saviour
When lost in the silk street by the sea
Who beat the path for Paul to walk upon
In the old heaven of Ayurveda,
Iron bhasma, stuffed mussels and tantric sex
Put aside dreams and Castaneda.
He sold his soul to the cannibal world of advertising
Saw his destiny in slight curves and scruffy clothes.
She spat equality,
Read books
And put Paul under a microscope.

Paul scorned,
Paul laughed and Paul said —
Romance, we'll see what marriage does to it, no?

Paul fled to the little continent
Paused for breath and
Ended his search.
Paradise
The green isle of a Dutch regime
The sweet cane and the sweetest women
Paul's searching blue eyes
Weary
Of thick Czech ankles and Slavic bones
Widened and gleaned the delicate contours
Of the bird of paradise.
The iridescent glow of the tropics
Bathed her feathers
Batak bred, Bach and bible versed

Dalima,
Slender bones
Beautiful thoughts;
Dalima has crept into my soul.
Eating my bones,
Gnawing at my senses,
Paul cried.
Dalima of the midnight world
Dalima
The Sumatran vision of my life
Teach me the Batak language and
I'll teach you English
Or whatever

We'll sing the song of love
Let the curtains rise.

Paul the lover
Nuclear Physics forgotten
Czech ballads
And Chopin waltzes now throb
With the exuberance of a butterfly heart,
Soaring mercury in barometer veins.
Wise and worldly,
Married and old,
We knew
When in love
Even gutters have green banks
Silvery ripples
Endless delights.

A Baga Imprint

I

Flaming
A tongue of yellow
darted.
Searching
Probing
The flaming deep.
The aching hips
the swollen lips.
Waves rose.
Drain the fire.
Swallow the heat,
the tumultuous seed.

Hope.
An unvoiced desire
to create
to nourish
a golden being
for a brief while.

II

Bleached bone-dust
of some ancient deep.
Rimming the ocean eye
damming the great salt tears.

Holding on
even when awashed
and sometimes drowned
by the waves.
That never cease to try
to escape.

Locked
in a mindless mating,
grain and grain
and grain and grain
each separate
each indistinguishable
from the other.
No memories.
No dreams.
No fears.
No desires.
No pain.

When flung
trodden
or shifted
by a careless wave
still intact
still content.

III

The sun beating the retreat
let the folds
of the ocean bed
climb higher and higher

till what
remained
was a smudge
staining the skies;
some bruised clouds
memories adrift
of a presence
lost
and a strange unbearable
emptiness.

Then
from the waves
rose a bridge
between the land of the living
and the city of the dead.
Coral-studded
Golden-beamed
Pearl-railed
beneath which fish serenaded
and dolphins waltzed.
From the spot
where the sun's blood was spilt
it spread
to the tips of your feet

Step on it
if you dare
where the dead and the living meet.
Entwining secrets
dreams
wisdom

hope.
Brush a cheek.
Touch a finger.
Walk
through a corridor of time.
Only for a moment
blink
and then nothing remains.

IV

Cashew grease.
Blackened boats.
Toothy urchins.
Shaven armpits.
Footprints in the sand.
Copulating beach benches.
Mussels in white wine. Mussels masala. A mussel shell
chalice.

Motorbike Vikings.
Hippies turned plutocrats.
Sleeping dogs.
Long shadows.
Naked babies.
Wind muscle.
Sea salt. Sea breeze. Sea that stills the horizon.

Hairy armpits.
Romping dogs.
Bobbing heads.
Lone towels.
Knotted fishing nets.

Old men aching to die.
Waves pounding. Waves retreating. Waves cast with golden bellies turning.

Swooping crows.
Perfect navels.
Plastic flip-flops.
Pineapple vendors.
Fisherman netting sand.
Mermaids in sarongs.
Sun tiring. Sun drooping. Sun dreaming of the morning.

Two men on a rock.
Looming cliff side.
Curving bay.
Cloud burst.
Salt stains.
Ocean trapped in a shell.
Beach in shadows. Beach brimming with brine. Beach at rest.

Crescent of the coconut pubis.
Twinkling light house.
Bent cigarette butts.
Squealing pig.
Ghost boat.
Juggler practising.
The sigh of the sea. The sigh of the sand. The sigh of the sun.

Malabar Mind

In his eyes, the lunatic gleam
"Ta ta Madras, ta ta fiends of hell
Keep your lady politicians and diseased flies."
The Malabar Mail wheezes and chuckles,
Look at this girl, the lunatic stares,
Her curves are ripe melons
Pardon me, I know not what I think,
May I touch your feet?
Please
My madness will vanish
With the soft breeze.
Let me go, I am not mad
Only deprived
Why did I leave the emerald cave?

The river Nila
Sand banks rising yellow and gritty
Once flourished triangular hate.
The cow worshippers, the pig haters
And the sunshine-haired cow eaters.
No one knows how it came about.
A thousand men piled into a carriage
Trundled and truckled, gasping for life.
When they opened the doors,
The stench, they say
Made people gag a mile away.

In Malabar, they cannot forget,
Sometimes the soft breeze smells of blood.

The Zamorin saw his face
On a piece of glass
Opened doors to colonial greed.
We have so much pepper,
So many spices.
Give it to them for mirrors.
Should man live a stranger to his face?
Our men now sail the seas
Across the bay to the desert Hope
In the backwaters, women sail
Lonely rafts, spinning coir, weaving dreams.

Zubeida, creature of the grimy hovel
Queen now of a green mansion
Fish juices trickle down her chin every day.
Is there more to life? She asks.
Geeta has her husband's voice on tape
The children listen to it now and then
Venu, distant cousin
Loves her on Wednesdays and Fridays
Satiating lust and a need to be held.
He caresses her skin.
She licks his eyes and wills him
To take her in rhythmic ecstasy.
It is only till 'he' comes back home,
She tells God.

Malibar
Manibar
Mulibar

Munibar
Malibar
Melibar
Minibar
Milibar
Minubar
Melibaria
Malabria*
Where the rain hisses
Echoes of a thousand footsteps.
Each seeking to measure the girth of wetness.
Eaves drip countless forsaken thoughts
Tiles splay revealing parted rafter thighs.
Politics is a way of life
Belong to a party
For an identity
The Congress or the RSS
The Muslim league or the Communists.
There is still about life here
A quiet air of restfulness.
Nayadi knee deep in slush
Tractors and buffaloes his companions.
Together they watch time amble by.
How can man be content
When he knows his rights?
Militants dressed in school teacher guises,
The forest hides disenchanted hearts
Madness threatens to erupt at any time.

Lying in the limpid green pool
Mouth open to catch the first dew drop.
Grandfather's concubine died yesterday.

Who will light his lantern at night? I wonder.
Father came back from roaming the plains,
Built a home and settled his books.
Mother likes to think of nothing.
The emerald cave has a soothing clutch.
The devil bird weeps: Poo-ah, Poo-ah.
I kiss my elephant hair talisman.
Coconut palms rustle their fingers.
Courage and the soft breeze
Will cure madness, they say.

Malabar was once a British district. After Independence, Malabar as a district was no longer recognized and the region was divided to form the northern part of what is today called Kerala. Though Malabar has no geographical boundaries, no presence on a map of India, it still exists as a state of mind.

*From A.D. 522 to the eleventh or twelfth century, Malabar was also called these names.

Happenings on the London Underground

It happened on the District line…

One blistery blustery February day
Mr. Patel crept from his council flat
dreaming of sunshine in a far away land
hugging close to heart sandwiches and a thermos
Mr. Patel sought escape.
From the dim confines of the restaurant tables,
squabbles, noises and the mounting bills at home.

Past Westminister, the tube rushed
a dank metal caterpillar bursting its sides.
He read the poem at Earl's Court
smiled at a poster of Petticoat Lane
And, at every stop, the mysterious gloomy voice
of God spoke — Mind the Gap.
Mr. Patel felt the corners of his mouth bloom.
Rushing past old men and preening water birds
around the grimness of the pond tourists shot
    photographs of.
Mr. Patel rushed for a place in the make-believe sun.
Before the easels were set up and strays wandered in,
curling his mittened hands, he pondered on life thus:
Did I do right by leaving home?
Did I sin by crossing the seas?
When the blood in his bones ceased to congeal like gum

Mr. Patel munched his sandwiches and sniffed the
earthy loam.

On the tube back home, Mr. Patel deep in reverie
offered a pound to a white beggar boy
the clink of coin in the outstretched can
for a minute, made him forget the indignities
to his ego, soul and mortal being.
God knows how Mr. Patel could do it
in these hungry times of recession and recycled nostalgia
A few flakes of snow fell.
Mr. Patel felt the content of a day spent well.

It happened on the District line…

Rosa Mundi

Marmalade mornings.
Dew licks its lips on rose petals.
A timid river crawls, pauses, crawls
through pepper wreathed arecanut groves.
A striated green land unfurls
when gates open.
A book slumbers
waiting to be woken and loved.
April blossoms in November and June.
Steam rises from a blue tea mug.
God is in heaven
The geese are in the pen
All's well with the world.
Rosa Mundi opens its eyes.

Rum and cola nights.
Paint daubs the skies.
Burnt sienna and ashes of rose.
The woods shiver.
The day is reluctant to leave.
Tempted to linger when pasta twirls
with crushed garlic, basil and sun dried memories.
Fireflies drizzle light.
Crickets shake their maracas.
Joshua chews on a bone.
Tom's asleep. Petra draws in her claws.

A pool of light scented with beedi smoke.
Rosa Mundi counting time.
As roses die and bloom.

Why Women Dream

I sell space,
Mortar, brick and
aluminium sliding windows.
Flats cost 960 per square foot
making telephone calls and
endless calls:
"Hello, can I help you?"
Travel faceless in buses,
wrapped sandwich-like in
college election posters.
My belly pinched,
crab claws grip and tug.
I search for a face,
beady eyes,
several pairs meet mine:
bastard, I swear softly.
No one hears me.
Suffer in silence,
the shame of it,
for being treated like a fair
piece of flesh.
The conductor has no change
He likes my face,
gives me the ticket.
The man behind me growls in disgust.
Privilege and pain

come together.
Love and aching
are the Gemini twins.

The roads are dark
the sky a midnight blue.
Street lamps cast more shadows than light.
I avoid one road.
Yesterday,
a little dog lay there.
Its snout in the drain.
Whining.
I stopped,
wanted to save it,
Hold it to my bosom, nurse it,
love it.
My beloved,
pricked pins
on my ballooning hopes.
The angel has a marble heart.
Very reasonable too,
Where could I take it?
Who would look after it?
I left it to die.
Guilt eats me like cancer,
sorrow in spasms.
I wish to live
in poppy fields,
lie in a red field of sleep,
love all the strays
and cliff-hangers,
breath in beauty

and senses that bloom.

House grows upon house,
open windows are peep holes.
The lady wears a red silk caftan.
Her husband holds to him
the Lhasa that goes on scooter rides.
The bed is unmade, rooms
dusty. Dinner is yesterday's leftovers,
the first hot meal.
Squirrels that scamper up trees
are lively.
They live as they should.

The wings of Pegasus ail and
shrivel. My beloved lies, bolster-like,
beside me.
Warm, wide open arms,
I turn to my side.

Free Fall

I like my body to be loved
touched, stroked and desired.
I am a woman who lives to fulfil
her nerve-end longings.
I paint these days
splashes of colour:
a lone fish
three women in brown.

My home is an embryo
faceless feet roam restlessly above and below.
My husband is busy climbing
his way up to loneliness.
The mail box gushes junk mail and family pleas.
My children are ferns in pots.
They demand little from me
Opening fists into my face.

Sometimes I dream
and dream some more:
I splash in a rock pool
breath beneath water
discover coral gardens and secret caves
take a merman lover
go underwater
live life, free fall.

I Want

I want to sit beside you in a rowdy dingy pub
Legs dangling, shoulders jostling, knees touching
I want your breath to drain the sweat off my brow
And for you to lick the bitterness off my lips
I want your eyes to seek mine
I want to hear the hushed lust in your voice amidst the noise.

I want to sit beside you in a dark balcony
Where yesterday's washing doesn't flap its crackling wings
I want us to hear the night call
Watch shadows play ball and time creep up a celestial wall
I want your fingers to unerringly seek mine
I want to exist as more than a mere habit.

Transgressions

This is for real
the weight of this hand
that gathers me to the curve of a hip
and so as I lie
in this nest of bed clothes and slumbering flesh
I tell myself
this warmth is content.
The rest —
the foolish leaping of a vagrant heart
at a look exchanged
across a room crowded
with people and objects;
the feel of fleeting skin;
the ripening of hunger
will not transgress into tomorrow.

What is This?

This must
be it then:
the derangement

of all senses...
when you breathe
the Giorgio

pulsing my pulse points
and I am drunk
on the whisky

you sip
between mouthfuls
of espresso.

* * *

Words crawl
And hiss
between us.

What
we dare not...
our syllables do:

with abandon
with naked joy,
they arch their necks

a ritual
to consummate
this intensity

so much more
than mere
desire.

* * *

I give you
my hand
to clasp.

I give you
my cheek
to kiss.

I give you
my dreams
to remember me by.

Sleepstar

Thinking
of you,
sleep
trickled
from between
my closed eyes
crept
and climbed
the skies
till it found a vacant space
to hang itself
from;
six-pronged
there
it stays
so that
you know
every night
is
for me
a sleepless night.

The Deciding Day

I walk to the lake
where the moon
kills itself
night after night
no bloated corpse
rises and floats
no inquests
no obituaries
no mourning
I turn
I think
I see you
leaning against a tree
arms crossed
eyes glinting —
I think I hear
you say
I couldn't leave;
mirages occur
in arid lands
in intense times
in extreme conditions
like deserts
and loneliness
the breeze dribbles wisdom
on my shoulders
and into my ears.

Hello Lust

I should have seen lust when it came calling
I should have known by now.

For it visits you
shaking little bells at the door
fragrant of sunshine, grass and sly desires.

For it trails a feather down your soul
and kneads your catatonic heart
and sends little pulse notes to your brain.

For it gathers you into its arms
and stifles the uncertainties of everyday.
And then gazes into your eyes and plants itself there.

For it promises you nothing
and leaves you adrift on a line
counting time with a slowly mounting heap of 'whys'.

For later it pretends it never was there
and all that happened was a state of mind
best forgotten and tossed aside.

You Said, I Agreed

Let us be friends, you said
Let us be friends, I agreed.

Let there be nothing more, you said.
Let there be nothing more, I agreed.

I made no declarations, no promises, you said
You made no declarations, no promises, I agreed.

It was a minor aberration, a detour, you said.
It was a minor aberration, a detour, I agreed.

It isn't as if I did anything, you said
It isn't as if anything happened, I agreed.

We came out of it with dignity, you said.
We came out of it with dignity, I agreed.

A Brief Respite

Wave after wave
of lunch
of bitterness
of love gone asunder
of aloneness
of matings
of silences
churned
and churned some more.
Rushing up in a giant heave
only to be
sucked away
by waters
that gurgled and giggled
at such human fatuousness
at such emotional debris.
Empty
exhausted
I stare into the mouth
of the toilet bowl
where all the oceans
of the world have gathered.
For now
the world has stilled.
For now I carry
no traces of the past.

Co-dependent

On that first afternoon
In the buttery yellow light
Of vanilla coloured walls
And coffee-breath-stained window panes
Your mouth shaped
Words, blessings and much hope.
Such perfection couldn't be without a flaw.
I was even then a weary acolyte, you see.
And so I searched your hands
For that visible shake
The handcuffs of some dependency.
You smiled as if you knew
And let your fingers rest on the table,
long, square tipped, quietly steady.

The next time
Light streamed
An ochre of a curry gone rancid.
You told me of razor blades and white lines
Ferried through intestines and cut with rat poison.
Of barren landscapes stoked with colour
And peopled with reasons to go on.
It was too much of an effort, you said
To keep this a secret
I bring with me, you said
A spent body and dammed-up mind.

On that last afternoon
All was yellow and still.
You had tried, you said
To kill the white habited monk.
Your fingers danced
And told me tales of withdrawal.
I saw you look at the payphone
An unbidden sigh escaped
Fetid and foul, every goodness wiped out of you.
I placed a coin on your palm.
I would rather see you dead than decay.
Here make that call, I said.

The House is Waiting

In the late hours, the woman sat.
A glass lamp, an egg, spilled its yolk of light.
She gnawed
Flesh of her thumb
The one that guided her pen
Through pages and life and many uncertain hours.
She pondered
If it would have been any different
If the house, the empty house,
in the scope of divine conjunctions
Streaked with tears, fears
and questions of what next,
Had been filled with a family
Of planets determined to cast content.
Instead she had this house,
That urged her on
To probe and seek
To bleed and stifle her pain
This empty house,
a house in waiting.

* * *

The house is old.
How old, no one knows.
Nobody remembers.
But the house has always been there.

The mottled red tiles.
The sagging wooden beams.
The cold floor
Beneath which maledictions lie.
Ghouls doomed
To crouch within copper pots.
Counting movements of the earth
By the cracking and splintering
Of lives that once lived above.

Brown, crumbly stone
Circles the house.
Stone that has seen
Many rains, much living.
In the October storms,
The ancient trees sway and creak.
Silver blades of lightning
Slice the black hardened tar
Old crones flailing their arms at the skies.

The air is sweet and cloying.
Smell it for yourself. You can if you try.
The mango blossoms,
The drying hay
And the rotting leaves on the ground.
Take my hand
Let's seek the soul of the house.
Do your eyes mist like mine do?
Termites have feasted
Chewed the vigour
Out of windowsills and rafters.
Invisible hands have spread

A mat of brown dust
Legions of spider slaves
Craft tapestries of filmy cobwebs.

If you listen carefully
You can hear voices.
Not the beating of our hearts
Or the creaking of spent wood
But the echoes of they who were here once.
Do you understand
Why I feel the way I do?
Tell me, do you wish to know
Who lived here?
What they ate, what they drank,
What they wore, what they thought,
Whom they loved?
Turn around and you will see what haunts me.

The house.
Silent and motionless.
The house. Eyes closed
as if it wishes to see no more,
know no more.
Mouth closed.
Resisting.
From its nose
that points to the sky,
no clouds of breath emerge.
For all you know the house could be dead.
Or, waiting.

* * *

The house peopled her strength

Filled her day and defined hopes.
And yet in the night a want unfurled;
to be a woman, a wife and no more.
The long shadow of an empty house.

The woman closed the pages
Shut the doors of the house
Braided her hair
Wiped her cheeks
And crept into bed.
There was no escape
from the house
But at least she had this.

The Lullaby

Between the door and the floor
There is a crack, harsh and lean
I wait for it to fill with substance —
The texture of my eyelid,
The color of burnt sienna —

Hush my baby, hush, don't you cry

Sipping at a glass of white wine
Rocking rhythmically
I kiss and let go the brow of my child
And ponder on this strange failing of men
Of wanting crevices filled, gaps closed and needing to
be held.

Hush my baby, hush, don't you cry

The door opens and allows a beam of light
I watch friends pour in, chalky faces, treacley voices,
Bearing crab claws chastened into petals
And lilies drooping already with homesickness.
I stretch my face into a smile willing them to go
And return to my sweating glass of dry consolation.

Hush my baby, hush, don't you cry

Rain creeps down the window pane
in reptilian slithers. The wind whips
The Jacaranda tree is shorn

And I let the day fall on my anger
Daddy's going to come by and by.

Hush my baby, hush, don't you cry

Neglect is a habit you need to learn young
Or, like me, in the downy confines of your bed
You'll have to let yourself be held, caressed and even
  subjugated
A kind of a whore, I trade my body
So that at night, I don't have to dream alone.

One Sunday Evening

Sipping wine from chunky glass tumblers;
couldn't find anything else.
Switch on a tape
someone's left behind in the video.
Arlo's on television
from so many years ago.
Half a million people
and mind music.
Across the night in the scrap yard jungle,
old cars lie waiting.
The moonlight glints on bent fenders.
The guitarist's sweaty back.
See see, Mac says
You're not seeing, Mac says.
Talk about it.
Think about it.
Don't just sing along.
A voice on the video.
A little girl played in the jeep
that came to stay yesterday.
Joan Baez's forgotten by Dylan.
Why can't you give up loving?
Her hair is all shorn,
but her voice haunts.
Joan Baez singing at Woodstock.
You were just a kid then, Mac says.

The kitchen smells of soup.
And pine disinfectant.
Let's get high tomorrow I say.
Four days ago
we could have had an orgy.
Now we're just a couple.
Three days from now
I'll have ghosts for company.
Last night
the party next door
brought Lennon
into our dreams.
See me, touch me, feel me, Mac sings.
Listen to it, he sings.
Wish I could
sail on an eyelash
in his eye.
See me as he sees me.
It's only half past eight.
Not keeping a journal.
Only a stream
of meaningless words.
Don't stop, Mac writes in curling loops.
Indian gurus and rock n' roll;
Neil Young's singing;
dogs lick sheep;
Kundalini yoga;
His hands seek the guitar.
In the afternoon I cried.
He and the blue sky saw me.
The mason putting his son's pants

out to dry stared.
Why am I not there? Mac cries.
I hold his hand and listen to the rain.
The beat.
On the TV,
men slide into slush,
heads locked in envelopes.
Split screen images of so much ecstasy.
Oh, Oh, oh, ooh, the chant goes on.
Tantric sex or the lotus position,
the couple there are making love.
'Wanna take you higher.'
Sing along.
There's blood in my heart.
Crosby Stills & Nash.
All this will end tonight.
Why did you end like that, Mac asks.
Snuggle deeper into my skin.
The man on TV's at his best.
Port-o-san,
portable loos.
Sure beats the woods.
The wine's over.
He's happy.
He's made only friends.
I fell in love.
Do I have a right to joy?
Am I allowed to cry?
My head lolls, a broken doll.
Voices sing to stop
the massacre at Vietnam;

Maybe, after all, the stars will come
out tonight and there will be love;

I look at Mac. Again and again. And over again.

Rain

Rain eludes me
Rain always has.

I watch the skies
Holding the window bars of an upper room
Bubbled, cracked, silver-crusted nevertheless
Through which once I saw love
At the tip of a cigarette butt.

I wait
For the heave, the tremble, the sting
Of the shy raindrop. For wetness
To lash and cleanse and raise
the loamy scent of a flesh long gone to sleep.

Rain eludes me
Rain did then.

Another room
Cow-like gray clouds amble inwards
At night it falls in stealthy drips
Into plastic buckets placed around our bed
Where love flung bedclothes over its head.

In the morning
I watch my rain wash the bathroom floor
Trickle and sing down a drain
Carrying with it to ground

The crumbling mortar of a dream.

Rain eludes me
Rain I can capture and hold.

In this new home
The brown of my eye mates
With the black of a crow's wing
My rain will come calling here
Take heed, an inner voice prepares me.

The rain comes,
Brings with it the shadow of choice
Step into the wetness of my embrace
You can't stay dry on a threshold
and yet be part of me.

Rain eludes me
Rain that I knew to be gentle once.

These days,
I hear the rain knock at the window pane
Beg, plead, let me in
I close my eyes, shut my mind
...rain, rain, go away...

It is enough I know the rain lives
That in some distant horizon it thrives.
Some times I think I feel the rain
When the avocado tree hums with bloom
Drizzling sap beneath a cloudless April sky.

The Face Mask

With sandal and turmeric dust
Yogurt gone a drippy sour
And a few drops of rose-watered hope
I fashion for myself
a splendid new face for this new me.

With this mask I will
Exfoliate the past speckled with yellow 'maybes'
Seep within and gather the debris of rejection
Smoothen weary pathways
And cleanse all traces of devastating faint praise.

Love for a Cat Man

Now I remember:
A crackling crept
through the room.
I cocked my head
And let it pass.
There was nothing there, I knew.

A coal moved
On sock clad toes
I echoed the flame
Outside by a pan of red embers
Cat man warmed his hands
Prometheus stealing my fire within.

II

Has someone told you this:

Cats eyes don't reveal much
Even as claws unsheath
And the pounce hurls unbidden.

Your eyes crinkle like a cat's
A cat playing with prey
A cat wanting to purr.

III

My cats live on a wooden shelf

Bronze, wood, steel and ceramic
And the Murano.
Large and fragile
With an arched back
And an orange fish within.
You, I think
Robber and keeper
My fire in frozen glass.
How do I reach through
Without shattering the glass?
Splintering a whole?
Tell me, Cat man
At what price the fire?

Next Monet

The boulders wore wet crowns
Where the murkiness had paused.
On a flash lit road we walked.
Fog blanketing us from reality.
My words your colours.
I stretch my fingers.
Then curl them into a fist
For now all I can
Is tease you — Next Monet?

Later I wait
Willing the morning to part
For you to knock on the door.
Ashes of the night sprawled on the grass
A pan of yesterdays smoking
The whisky bottle chuckles on its side.
If you do come, I promise to not call you
The Next Monet…

When I pour milk on my cereal.
You whisper: I came by. Where were you?
Milk sops the cereal and hurt
But the wind swirls the words away.
You paint a picture with your breath:
The bed by the window, a tub in the kitchen,
a door on wheels, birds singing and I think: if I get there,
You will be more than the Next Monet.

An Ostrich's Love Song

Fight your own battles.
If you win, I'll rejoice
With you in your triumph and glory.

If you lose,
You have the solace,
Of hiding your head between two pillows.

The Highway

Tarmac ribbons
Tires roar
Miles are crunched and swallowed whole.
Smoke clouded windows frame landscapes.
Greens and browns that stretch and wait.
Sun smears, shadows pace.
Wind fingers furrow hair.
Tossing a syllable, a sound from speeding
    conversations.
Gathering ends of words for strange ears.
Lights speak
As they dip and flash.
Or blind
A cat skewered in mid motion.
Skid marks that speak of lost control.
Eyes in the ground that glow in the dark.
Go on, go on, milestones urge.
It's not the destination, it's the going.
Read the signs
And follow the course.
Tarmac ribbons
Tires roar
Stay on the highway all night long.

The Last Rites

Whitescapes,
Ceilings, walls, starched cotton sheets, crisp uniforms.
You lie there
Staring into the whiteness beyond this white
Wistfully.
Tubes meander, this way and that, in and out,
Breathing life, pumping blood,
Feeding sustenance, draining rivulets of flesh.

Wood from the house you lived,
doors, rafters, gargoyle bed.
When did it enter your soul?
Wedging us apart forever.
Look at me,
Part your lips, raise a finger, twitch a nerve,
Show me in some way, you wish to go on
Trapped in splinters of teak.

Lean back in the green armchair
Where you liked to sit spooning wisdom into my
    reluctant throat.
Let me cloak you with rainbows,
And tiny mirrors that let loose a galaxy of stars.
Let me brush your hair into a million waves.
There you are, as you used to be, no tubes, no distress,
    no borrowed life.

I'll hold your hand as you let go.
Exhale. Exhale.
A beam of light? A golden stairway?
A topaz tunnel? A vortex of black?
Whatever there is, keep going,
Beyond it is hope someday we shall meet.
Until then,
Go in peace, Grandmother.

An Investment of Faith

Zuleika screamed.
The brown and white goat shook its head and stared.

'Thousand strips of palm leaves,
have been,' Mad Moidu said,
'twisted, turned and shaped.
Here they lie:
mats, fans and elongated trays.
Do you see how the sun's rays
as they glide over the palm leaf ware
turn our yard into a wave of light?'
Mad Moidu beamed.
'Look at the miracle happening at our feet.'

'Suleiman's Dirhams should go
Not into gold chains or making our walls glow.
What we never had,
we can't miss.
Now look at this Zuleika.
Isn't this what we dream about?
The sea of abundance,
the hope of plenty,
Eternal life, the arrival of golden light,
All woven into strips of a thousand palm leaves.

In the palm leaf glimpse the passage of time,
lemony summer, the monsoon damp,

sunshine, winter night.
Once it made frantic gestures to the clouds,
Now it rests,
rustling, gossiping, at our feet.
What celestial secrets it must know
To bewitch the unruly dust so.
See how meekly the ground lies
Tamed and enchanted by its immigrant sighs.

The satin smoothness of its skin
tempts my hand to linger.
Hidden in its every strand is the memory of life.
Alive and breathing.
Dead and dazzling.
The real and the corporeal, all together, all at once
In this message from God to man,
All of Suleiman's Dirhams have found expression.
Companion, wife, mother of Suleiman,
Tell me for once, I have done right.'

Zuleika screamed
A wordless renting of the air:
'All of Suleiman's Dirhams gone
How could you Mad Moidu?'
The brown and white goat skipped,
hopped and jumped a bush,
Leaving in its trail
a chorus of little bleats
Mad Moidu's done it again,
Mad Moidu's done it again.

Flash-tale

The night of the noon the boy fell
heaved by a mysterious hand
an electric wire shearing his throat
a cement block slamming his life;
red driblets of heat staining
the undersides of his still twitching feet
and shattered glass screams,
a firefly appeared.
A spark in the dark hallway.
As if to say:
I was this and no more
And yet I was this.

That night water crept up the pipes
in stealth and shame.
Candles in homes kept
a frenzied wake
Through the stairwell and shadows
the firefly winged
Trailing its flash tale.
So that all who saw
would never forget the boy who fell,
the day Saturn moved into Taurus.
Silent screams remain etched.
Zigzags of light

Words Will Never Cease to Sing

Every year
I climb the stairs
As if I were a pilgrim
Bearing in my eyes
Black bundles
Of unwashed sin
A year's forbidden trespasses
A year's foolish indulgences.

Every year
The doctor peers into my past
Through the eye of a gauge;
I try to read
The timbre of his voice
When he speaks:
Which one is brighter?
The green or orange orb?

Every year
An ingrown nail prods at my fear
Is the orange orb
The flame of the sunset
Or the curve of the inner eye lid?
Is the green the emerald of home?
Or the dull ache of
Verdigris on bronze?

Every year
I pray for respite
that my answer
Will somehow be right
That the darkness
Threatening, looming
A swarm of furious bees
Shall not settle in my eyes.

Every year
I ask: Is there someone
Whose eyes are worse than mine?
He leans back in the chair
doodles on a pad
There is one, but
Why talk about these things?

II

I have wondered
In the stillness of the dawn
In narrow crouching lanes
Where dark and silence
Walk hand in hand
If this is what will be …
When truth shall no longer be seen.

That the truth I can't see
Will slip between my fingers
And all that shall remain
Will be the music, false companions,
Tripping unseeing from my finger tips.
For the words

Shall cease to sing.

III

This morning
I sought you
Not knowing what it was
I sought;

What shall I seek
From a shrine?
What shall I learn
From a silence?

The hospital room
The cold sterile whiteness
Echoed a thousand words
Ghosts of the children

You let free to gambol.
Your eyes held me by my throat
Trapped those fugitive words
That sought to escape.

Later,
When it was time
To leave
Your eyes smiled into mine.

And the strength of your grip
Said all that I wanted to hear.
I carry with me
As if it were a benediction.

— We have to pay a price

For who we are
I entombed in my silence
You in dwindling light.

But while all may cease,
The truth will never elude you and I
Words will never
Stop singing for us.

The Soldier's Song

I walk the khaki hills
I hide in deep furrows of land
I write letters to my family
I tell them all is well.
I drink my tea
I polish my rifle
I try not to think
I block out fear for it cripples.
When I spot an intruder
I do not look him in the eye
I shoot to kill.
One bullet for one enemy soldier.
This is what I'm taught
This is how I fight.

The Eleven o' clock News:

Green jagged toothed hills
A sky
An olive green truck raises dust
A soldier sits outside his tent
His foot wears a white badge of honour
His palms nurse a mug
His eyes say nothing.
Two other soldiers
Pose for the TV camera
hug each other.
Their valour drenches their smiles
"If you are watching us,
tell our families we are alive."

Lieutenant Jerry Premraj is dead
His 45 day old bride
To the wall she turns her head.
— oh why, oh why, oh why —
I sit, huddled frozen
My lips take up the chant of her cries
Two nights ago, a father says
The phone rang at midnight,
He died for his country, for us.
But tell me how do I
explain death, war or country
To my two-year-old grandson now.

The newscaster recites ratios:
The number of men injured, dead, missing
The number of battles won.
In villages and towns,
Phones ring with sepulchral tones
Telegrams are weighed down with death
Men die; martyrs are born
But the war must go on.

Later I trail the rooms of my house
The enemy they say
Have snow mobiles and fur lined boots
Expensive cigarettes and cream biscuits.
Our men have frost bitten toes
Feel a dull white fear ravage their bones.
In my home of plenty
I do not know what it is to want
I gave to the war relief fund
I spoke appropriate words
But what all this means
I have never known
till tonight.

I sit by my son who sleeps
His ivory face is untainted by fear, politics or hate.
At school, he traces the borders of our land
With a red pencil and a steady hand.

Twenty Fellows

— for *Amy Eshoo* —

The cows know
No need
For self expression.
To create, to conquer,
To crack the hourglass
With an indelible mark
That's one's own.
The cows stand still
Hoof deep in browning grass
Feel the sun brand their backs.
The cows don't care
How far the mountains of muse stand.

It is only us
Twenty Fellows huddled here
With stolen time from everyday lives
Who stare
At the mountains
Blue ridged against the blue sky.
Seeking in it a measure
Of our own worth.
That we know is in us.
All we need is to find
The trail to reach there.

Grasslands

— for *George Blecher* —

In the sun stained pasture
The cows live
Ruled by their four stomachs.
Eat. Shit. Whisk a tail.
Chew some cud
And some more.
Let the bull fuck you
In the only way he knows how.
Roll your eyes at the farmer
Probably he'll see you
As more than a little mark
He makes on a clipboard
Seated in his red trailer truck.
So that when the calf arrives
He'll let you keep it awhile.
The cow's only expression is its moo.

Rock Polishing Beneath the Chinese Elm Tree

— for *Rhoda Stamell* —

Imprints of some ancient time
Ancestors to some earthly being
Rest trapped
Beneath the skin of a rock.
Waiting for a pair of hands.
Three pie dishes lined with chamois.
Grades of ashen grit.
And fingers aching to rush.

Gnats hover
Impatient mothers wanting to know
What we see in the rocks.
Till we repel them
with our indifference
coated with brown vanilla extract.
Beneath our fingers
The naked rocks glow.

Sunshine

The Colony Cat

— for *Peter E. Murphy* —

There is nothing about her
That suggests
A ball of fire
Or a heap of living coals.
Tawny warmth
Or the radiance of self-containment.

She sits on the stone
Beneath the VCCA HOT L sign.
A register of comings and goings.
Waiting for the door to open
And a lonesome being to come her way.

For fingers that will trail
Course carelessly
Through black and white fur.
For soft crooning words
To envelop her
To calm her savage need to be loved.

Somewhere in her is a mew
That has yet to find its voice.
When the skies drizzle
Shooting stars

She searches for it with us.

For one she can pounce upon
Hold between her unsheathed claws
Toss and play
Roll and kill
Make believe it is the black snake
That like her mew escaped her.

A Gaggle of Gazebo Thoughts

— for *Neal Weiss* —

Viennese Actionists. The flight of a swan's neck. Blood on breasts. Blood from the womb. Blood in the mouth. Red pagan juices. People in evening clothes watch. Seeking continuity in nature. A revelation that great possibility waits in some other level of consciousness.

Nothing has moved you ever so much, you said.

An alpine climber whose toes exploded. The grandmother who waited for the toes to grow back. As if he was a giant lizard. The completeness of a solitary hiker. Body fluids, breath and foot steps merge into a single state. Leaping off a cliff side is the ultimate rush you said. What would you rather have? You ask: One breast? Or, one foot?

It'll give me an understanding of your values, you said.

Sunshine. Black snake. Shooting stars. Syl leaping in the air. Rhoda rock polishing. Lettuce shredding. Inner tube dancing by a pool bluer than the blue ridged mountains. Standing inside a sculpture and mooing. America in the library. Howl on the lawns. Bourbon stain glasses. Smoke that stretch curls of the mind. Popcorn crumbs. The guitar frets giggle.

Jaws of time crunch relentlessly on sunflower seeds, you said.